Parents and Caregivers,

Stone Arch Readers are designed to provide enjoyable reading experiences, as well as opportunities to develop vocabulary, literacy skills, and comprehension. Here are a few ways to support your beginning reader:

- Talk with your child about the ideas addressed in the story.
- Discuss each illustration, mentioning the characters, where they are, and what they are doing.
- Read with expression, pointing to each word. You may want to read the whole story through and then revisit parts of the story to ensure that the meanings of words or phrases are understood.
- Talk about why the character did what he or she did and what your child would do in that situation.
- Help your child connect with characters and events in the story.

Remember, reading with your child should be fun, not forced. Each moment spent reading with your child is a priceless investment in his or her literacy life.

Gail Saunders-Smith, Ph.D.

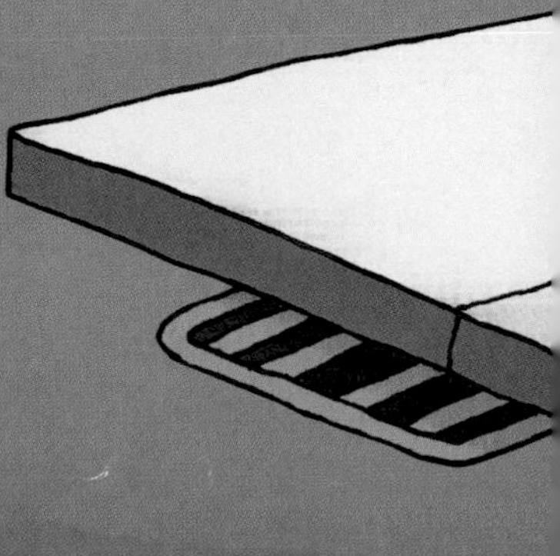

STONE ARCH **READERS**

are published by Stone Arch Books
a Capstone Imprint
151 Good Counsel Drive, P.O. Box 669
Mankato, Minnesota 56002
www.capstonepub.com

Printed in the United States of America in Stevens Point, Wisconsin.
102010
005972R

Library of Congress Cataloging-in-Publication Data
Crow, Melinda Melton.
Little wheels / by Melinda Melton Crow ; illustrated by Patrick Girouard.
p. cm. – (Stone Arch readers)
ISBN 978-1-4342-1865-0 (library binding)
ISBN 978-1-4342-2297-8 (pbk.)
[1. Trucks–Fiction.] I. Girouard, Patrick, ill. II. Title.
PZ7.C88536Li 2010
[E]–dc22

2009034286

Summary: Little Blue is too small for some jobs. Find out if he finds the right job for him.

Art Director: Kay Fraser
Graphic Designer: Hilary Wacholz
Production Specialist: Michelle Biedscheid

Reading Consultants:
Gail Saunders-Smith, Ph.D.
Melinda Melton Crow, M.Ed.
Laurie K. Holland, Media Specialist

THE PESKY PIGEON
Every time you turn the page, look for the pigeon.

LITTLE WHEELS

by Melinda Melton Crow

illustrated by Patrick Girouard

STONE ARCH BOOKS
a capstone imprint

This is Fire Truck.
This is Blue Truck.
This is Green Truck.
This is Yellow Truck.

"I am going to work," says Fire Truck.

STATION
5

"I will help you!" says
Blue Truck.

“You are too little to help me,”
says Fire Truck.

5

Fire Truck drives away.

5

"I am going to work," says Green Truck.

“I will help you!” says
Blue Truck.

"You are too little to help me,"
says Green Truck.

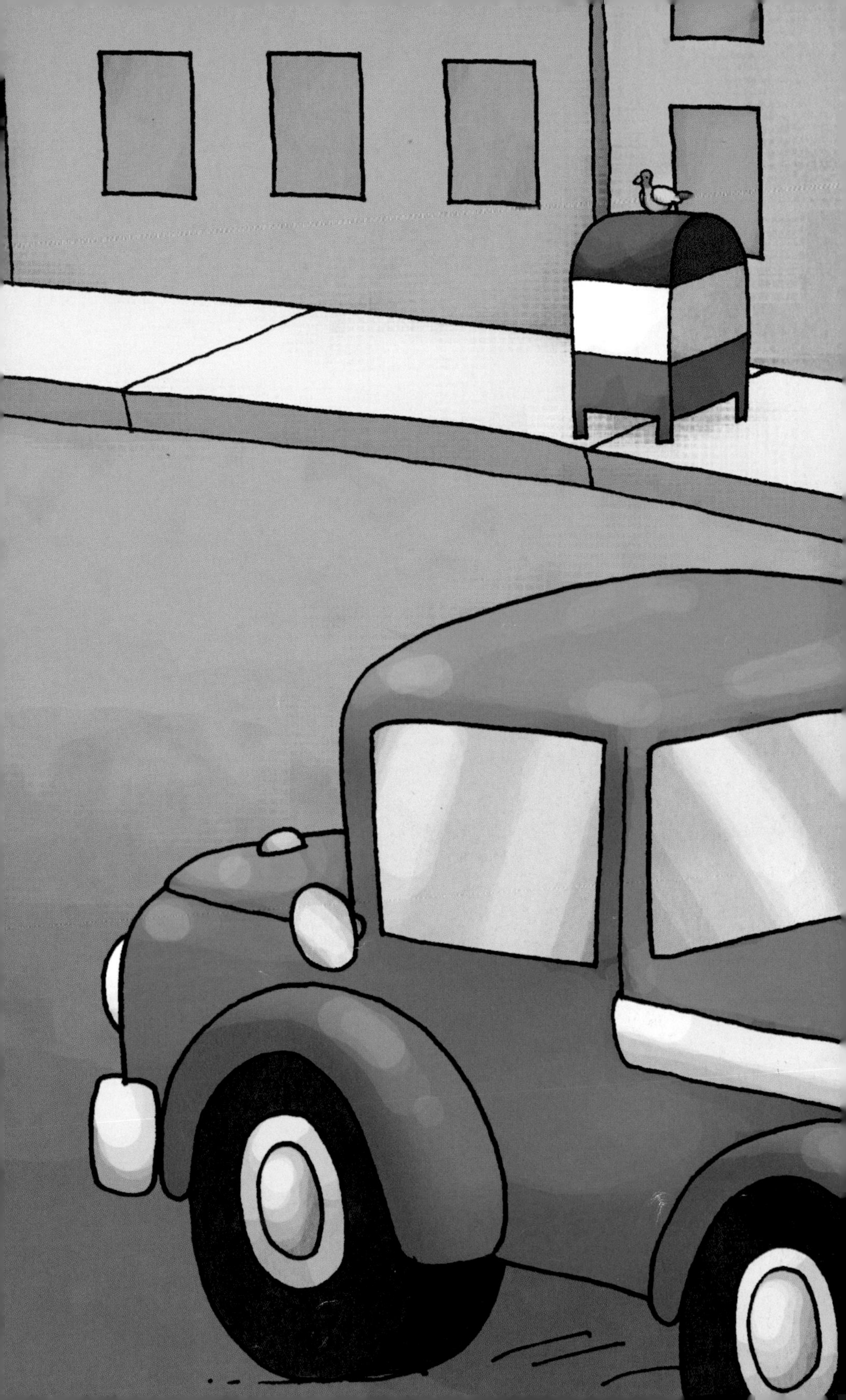

Green Truck drives away.

"Can you help me with this tree?" asks Yellow Truck.

"I'm too little to help,"
says Blue Truck.

"No, you are not," says
Yellow Truck.

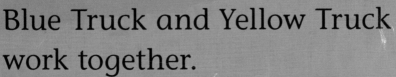

Blue Truck and Yellow Truck work together.

"I'm not too little to help!"
says Blue Truck.

STORY WORDS

work
help
little
drives
tree
together

Total Word Count: 115

Follow your favorite **TRUCK** pals as they **learn** about the open road.